D1258182

Monsters on Wheels

E. P. Dutton & Co., Inc. New York

Monsters on Wheels

written and photographed by George Ancona

HARDEMAN COUNTY LIBRARY
QUANAH, TEXAS

Photographs on pp. 38 and 39 courtesy of NASA

Text and photographs copyright © 1974 by George Ancona

All rights reserved. No part of this publication may be
reproduced or transmitted in any form or by any means,
electronic or mechanical, including photocopy, recording,
or any information storage and retrieval system now
known or to be invented, without permission in writing
from the publisher, except by a reviewer who wishes to
quote brief passages in connection with a review written
for inclusion in a magazine, newspaper, or broadcast.

Library of Congress Cataloging in Publication Data

Ancona, George   Monsters on wheels.

SUMMARY: Text and photographs introduce the physical
characteristics and functions of a variety of machines
designed for heavy labor. Included are the bulldozer,
tractor, crane, paver, and others.

1. Motor vehicles—Juvenile literature. 2. Machinery—
Juvenile literature.   [1. Motor vehicles. 2. Machinery]
I. Title.

TL147.A5   629.22'5   73-20308   ISBN 0-525-35155-8

Published simultaneously in Canada by Clarke,
Irwin & Company Limited, Toronto and Vancouver

Designed by George Ancona
Printed in the U.S.A.   Third Printing

To

Lisa

Gina

Tom

Isabel

&

Marina

Contents

Introduction

This book is about some of the strange monsters that have become part of our world. Had we lived during the Mesozoic era, a hundred million years ago, we would have been surrounded by dinosaurs. If these creatures were alive today, man would probably harness them and put them to work, as he has put the elephant to work in India.

Since this is not possible, man has had to create new monsters to perform the gigantic tasks that must be done every day in our modern civilization. More products than ever before have to be made and transported, more roads built, and more buildings constructed for our crowded world.

To meet these demands man has developed machines to push, lift, dig, crush and haul. And since man has the wheel, he can move these monsters to where the jobs must be done.

Many of these wheeled giants can be seen as they travel across the landscape, but others are used in out-of-the-way places such as docks and quarries.

This book has been organized to illustrate the sequence in which the machines are used in various industries. It begins with earth movers and machines used in road building. Next is the group of giants employed in shipping and cargo transporting. Some of the larger agricultural machines follow. Monsters of the construction field are next. The book ends with a wheeled machine used in man's exploration of space.

Scraper

Shown on the preceding pages is the Caterpillar 633 Scraper with its hydraulic elevating scraper system, a method that increases the capacity of the bowl by heaping the earth into it. The capacity of this model is 32 cu. yds. heaped, 72,000 lbs. of payload. It has a 415-hp forward engine, weighs 87,900 lbs., and measures 43 ft. 10 in. long, 12 ft. 6 in. wide, and 13 ft. high.

Above is the Terex TS-24 moving along without scraping. The blade is in a raised position. This model, which has a rear engine as well and all-wheel drive, has a capacity of 24 cu. yds. struck or level, 80,000 lbs. of payload. Two diesel motors provide 613-hp forward and a maximum speed of 29.6 mph. Empty, the TS-24 weighs 171,000 lbs. and measures 48 ft. long, 11 ft. wide, and 12 ft. high.

Man changes the surface of the earth to suit his needs. Every day new roads are built, large areas of land are cleared to make room for new buildings, and often the contour of the land has to be redesigned for these purposes.

Years ago this was achieved by the use of shovels filling buckets with dirt, carrying them elsewhere and dumping them. The scraper was devised to do all these jobs on an immense scale. This huge earth wagon scrapes the earth from high areas, carries it into low areas, and dumps it. Scrapers are used in road construction, landfill operations, strip coal mining, and land development operations. They come in many sizes, designs, and capacities. Two are shown here.

The operator sits in the front section, which is the tractor. Behind is the scraper with its bowl and cutting edge. On the larger scrapers an additional engine in the rear provides extra power. The two sections are united at one point so that they pivot for maximum flexibility over rough ground. It's an incredible sight to see these giants bending from side to side as they struggle over broken ground. Occasionally a bulldozer (pp. 12 and 13) will push from behind to provide better traction. Hydraulic power, achieved by forcing water or oil through a small opening, drives the blade of the scraper into the earth as it is pulled along. When the bowl is filled, the blade is raised, the bowl closed, and the earth taken to a lower area where it is dumped and spread to raise the level of the site. In this manner hundreds of miles of land have begun the change from wilderness to sleek ribbons of highway.

The bowl section of the TS-24 can heap as much as 32 cu. yds. of earth. Here the 10-ft.-wide blade is shown cutting into the earth. It can cut as deep as 1–1 1/2 ft. When ejecting the earth, it can spread it in a controlled manner to a depth of 2 ft. The steering and scraping functions are operated hydraulically.

Loader

A loader is basically a giant shovel on wheels. It's designed to dig into a bank, lift the earth, and dump it into a hauler or truck. Shown here is the Terex 72-81, one of the larger size front-end loaders. It has a "pivot steer" feature that enables the operator to maneuver in narrow spaces. The hydraulically operated bucket can lift 9 cu. yds. of earth and rock at a 45° angle, 13 ft. high for dumping.

This giant responds with amazing speed and articulation to the skilled operator, who must work the loader to its maximum capacity without abusing it. To watch a man controlling 115,000 lbs. with 465 gross hp is an impressive sight.

The bucket positions on a Terex 72-81 Loader (shown in the three photos above) are controlled by four hydraulic cylinders, two to lift and two to tip. For digging, the bucket is in the low position. The loader drives it into the earth and tips it up. Then the bucket is lifted over a truck and tipped to dump. A 35-ton truck can be filled with three buckets.

The advantage of using loaders on wheels is their maneuverability. The front-end pivoting allows for fast turnaround so they can be driven to the work site. Buckets are interchangeable for rock or general-purpose work. This Caterpillar 966 Front-End Loader is at work in a quarry. It has a 170-hp engine, is 22 ft. 6 in. long and 17 ft. 5 in. high with the bucket extended.

Hauler

These vehicles are designed to carry maximum payloads. Their size makes it impossible to move them over ordinary roads and bridges. These lumbering giants can be seen at various immense highway construction sites working together with loaders, moving in rows to dump tons of earth and rock into craters to change the land contours.

In quarries where power shovels fill them, haulers move tons of rock to the crushers; at mining sites, they carry tons of ore; and on salt flats they bring the raw salt to the processing plants.

The Euclid R-35 Rear Dump Hauler has a 12-cylinder, 434-hp, 2-cycle diesel engine. It is 27 ft. 9 in. long and 12 ft. 7 1/2 in. wide. At the cab guard, the highest point, it is 12 ft. 6 in. When it is being loaded to its 20-cu.-yd. capacity, the entire body shakes as tons of rock pour in. To absorb these shocks, the body is rubber-cushioned on the frame. With a payload of 70,000 lbs., the net weight is 128,300 lbs.

Bulldozer

At first glance a bulldozer seems out of place in a book about wheeled machines, since it is a track-type vehicle. But the wheels are there and many of them: two large ones and nine rollers on each side that guide the track. The bulldozer is a crawler tractor with a broad horizontal blade or ram attached in front. With this blade it can push, clear, gouge out, or level off land. The tracks provide powerful traction and often these machines can be seen working behind scrapers, pushing them out of soft ground.

Blades vary in design depending on the kind of job to be done. A bulldozer blade can loosen stubborn rock and dirt, push it to another location, then, angling the blade, slide the earth off sideways. A single lever operates hydraulically to raise, lower, tilt, or float the blade. Sometimes two of these monsters are attached side by side to a 24-ft. blade or one behind the other, doubling its pushing capabilities, and operated by one man.

Perched high in the cab, the operator (shown above) controls the blade with one right-hand lever. He controls the steering clutch levers, one for each track, with his left hand, and the steering brakes with his feet. He regulates speed with a hand throttle and a decelerator on the floor. This Caterpillar D9G Bulldozer has a 6-cylinder, 385-hp, turbocharged diesel engine. It is 23 ft. 3 in. long, 11 ft. 2 in. high, and 9 ft. 6 in. wide, and weighs 67,100 lbs. without the blade.

Working at a sanitary landfill site, the International Harvester TD25 Bulldozer pushes garbage into position to be covered by layers of earth. In landfill operations bulldozers share the work of scrapers and compacters. This crawler tractor weighs 54,000 lbs. and is powered by a 6-cylinder, 285-hp diesel engine.

The Caterpillar 825B Compacter has a 6-cylinder, 300-hp turbocharged engine and weighs 64,800 lbs. Its four 48-in. drum wheels have "sheepsfoot" tampers attached. The blade spreads out recently dumped fill earth and the drums compact it. The front two wheels and blade swivel together 44° left or right for better maneuverability. As haulers and scrapers dump their loads, the compacter follows behind, leveling the new dirt.

Compacter

Every day man produces tons and tons of garbage. How to dispose of it has become a major problem. One solution is sanitary landfill operations. Garbage trucks dump their loads into low areas where, after being crushed and compressed, it is covered over with earth. This "new" land is then developed into parks, golf courses, or building sites.

The job of compressing garbage is done by a compacter specifically designed for this purpose. It has four chopper wheels each with twenty steel blades welded on in a chevron pattern. These crush and chop the refuse in addition to providing better traction on uneven ground and steep inclines. Attached to the front end is a bulldozer landfill S-blade for spreading both refuse and earth. The high trash rack increases its capacity to 20 cu. yds. without blocking the operator's view. On this compacter, the Caterpillar 826B, the two front wheels and blade move together on a pivoting front end for greater maneuverability. An enclosed air-conditioned and heated cab protects the operator.

Compacters are also used in road construction or wherever earth has been used as fill. For this the machine has a "tamping foot" type of wheel with a fill-spreading blade in front. The vibration plus the weight of the machine pound and compress the earth, preparing it for grading.

The two front wheels of the Caterpillar 12F Grader can be tipped from side to side. This enables the long machine (26 ft. 10 in.) to make tighter turns and helps to stabilize it on steep banks. The blade is suspended from a geared circular frame which positions it at the desired scraping angle. The angle is determined by the density of the soil. This model has a 6-cylinder, 125-hp diesel engine and a 6-speed transmission. It weighs 26,700 lbs. The wheel lean, brakes, and steering are operated hydraulically.

Grader

After earth has been dug, moved, dumped, pushed, and compacted to a rough state, the graders come in to smooth and shape the land. Slopes must be contoured to carry away surface water into ditches to prevent erosion. For this job a 12-ft. blade is suspended in the middle of this giant insect-like vehicle. The blade can be revolved on either side of the frame to cut into a bank of earth at as much as a 90° angle. It can smooth the surface of the earth by moving back and forth along a roadway, and by gradually tipping its blade, increase the grade to a greater angle. At the edges of a roadway the blade is pitched sharpest to make runoff ditches.

18

This small paver, a Blaw-Knox PF-25, is capable of laying 8-ft.-wide strips of asphalt. It is powered by a 69-hp gasoline engine. The two front wheels are of solid rubber while the tires on the two drive wheels are pneumatic. The hopper is shown in the filled position. As the asphalt is deposited on the road, the two ends lift hydraulically to allow the material to flow.

Paver

In order to protect the surface of a new roadway from traffic and weather, a durable coating must be applied by a paver. Asphalt, a waterproof mixture of tar and sand or gravel, is one such coating material. A truck delivers hot asphalt to the construction site and deposits three tons of it into the front hopper of the paver. The paver moves slowly forward in a straight line, depositing a ribbon of asphalt on the roadway. Jets of flame keep the material pliable. The rear of the paver holds a platform that spreads the surface of the asphalt. This platform or screed can adjust to vary the depth of the asphalt from 1/4 in. to 6 in. Men following the paver level off any rough spots and smooth out the sides and joints.

Roller

Following right behind the paver is a vibrating roller that compacts the asphalt while it is still soft. In addition to the weight provided by the huge front drum, this model has a vibrating system that creates a dynamic force of 27,000 lbs. The rate can be varied by the operator from 1,200 to 2,300 vibrations per minute. To prevent the asphalt from sticking to the drum and smooth tires, water is sprayed through nozzles on them constantly. In winter, oil is mixed with the water. The front drum is steerable. Without the water sprays, the roller can be used to compact earth.

This RayGo Rustler 404B Vibrating Roller is 17 ft. 3 1/2 in. long, 7 ft. 11 1/2 in. wide, and 8 ft. 5 in. high. It weighs 18,300 lbs. and is powered by an 88-hp diesel engine. The drum is 84 in. wide and 59 in. in diameter. Two tanks under the operator's platform hold a total of 168 gallons of water for spraying the drum, through nozzles shown here, and through dual nozzles for each smooth tire.

Giant Fork Truck

This giant can raise 40-ft. containers weighing as much as 100,000 lbs. Instead of lifting from the bottom as a fork lift does, this truck has a frame that fits over the top of a cargo container and locks at each corner. It can now lift 9-ft. 6-in.-high containers, move them anywhere, and stack them three units high. Once a container is in position, the operator releases the locks and raises the frame, leaving the container in place. The frame can also move sideways for better alignment with the container.

An open container designed to hold four automobiles can be lifted easily and carried to a waiting truck, where it is lowered gently and precisely onto the truckbed. The truck will deliver the container directly to a showroom.

The FK50 Silent Hoist Liftruk seen here is designed for large-container handling. It weighs 95,000 lbs., is powered by a 225-hp gasoline engine, and can travel at speeds up to 15 mph. The two rear wheels are for steering while the four front wheels provide traction and drive.

23

Straddle Carrier

To cut down the time it takes to load and unload ships, an entirely new system of shipping cargo has been devised. Cargo is packed in containers at the factory and taken by truck to a port where it is weighed and sealed. A straddle carrier lifts the containers off the trucks and moves them to the outbound storage area. As two gantry cranes unload containers from a ship and place them on the dock, the straddle carrier picks them up and takes them to an inbound storage area where trucks call for them. After the inbound cargo is unloaded, the straddle carrier brings the outbound containers to dockside and the gantry cranes distribute them on deck according to weight. Using this system, ships can put to sea again in a matter of hours instead of days.

These straddle carriers are truly monstrous. Since the operator's vision is limited, one safety device is a constant tooting whistle that warns of their approach. To see and hear several working at the same time is an awesome experience.

Dwarfed by a gantry crane at dockside, this Clark Series 512 Van Carrier is 25 ft. 7 in. high, 13 ft. 4 in. wide, and 33 ft. 4 in. long. It can travel 17 mph empty and 12 mph loaded. It weighs 89,000 lbs. and can lift 67,200 lbs. All six wheels can be turned, making it exceptionally maneuverable. It is designed to carry containers 20–40 ft. long by hooking into each top corner of the container and lifting it hydraulically. The carrier can stack containers three high, but two high is more usual, since this enables the carrier to select a container from the center of a row, lift it, and move it out.

Piggy Packer

Sometimes it is more economical to ship a cargo container cross-country by train. A truck will deliver it to a rail freight depot, where the truck cab is detached, leaving the container on wheels. A loader called a Piggy Packer, which is 52 ft. high, wraps its four steel arms around the container and lifts it. With this huge load in the air, it drives to a railroad siding where an empty flatcar waits. The operator gently lowers the container into place while two men, one working on the ground and the other on the train, lock down the wheels. This operation calls for skill on the part of the operator and team-work by all three men. With a different front boom, the same machine is used for logging.

Tractor

As more and more people left the farm to work in the city, the farmer has had to produce larger crops with less labor to meet the growing demands of our industrial society. He has been able to do this by using more productive methods and laborsaving machines. The tractor has always been a part of the farm landscape but it, too, has grown in scale and capability over the years. One such giant, the turbo tractor, seen here pulling a 7-bladed plow, means that a farmer can now plow 90 acres in an 8-hour day instead of the 20–25 acres he used to plow, working late into the night. And this same tractor, with an assortment of front and rear attachments, can do other seasonal jobs such as harrowing, cultivating, tilling, planting, fertilizing, spraying, hoeing, mowing, raking, and harvesting. It is powered by a 175-hp turbo diesel engine, has a 13 ft. 6 in. turning radius, and can shift from 4-wheel to 2-wheel drive.

In the top picture the International Harvester 4166 Turbo Tractor is backing into the barn to hook up with a 7-blade trailing plow. Hoses are quickly connected to provide hydraulic steering for the plow wheels, which also adjust to the desired furrow depth. The circular disks alongside the blades cut into the earth, allowing the plow to turn the earth without clogging the blades. Should a blade hit a rock, it trips up and pops back into position. This model cuts seven furrows at one time.

Combine

At harvest time thousands of acres of corn must be cut, threshed, and stored. This task would be impossible without this very sophisticated combine. The machine does its numerous jobs right in the field, making it easier for the farmer to transport and store the grain.

Moving along a cornfield, the combine drives its pointed "corn heads" between the rows, gathering and cutting the stalks close to the ground. As the stalks fall into a spinning auger, they are snapped into small pieces and the heads are separated from them. The heads ride on long conveyors to spinning cylinders where the threshing takes place: the husks are removed and the kernels separated from the cob. The stalks, husks, and cobs are thrown out the rear of the combine to fertilize the field while the kernels, cleaned by air jets, are deposited in a grain tank that holds up to 112 bushels. When the tank is full, the combine deposits its load of grain in trucks waiting at the end of the field.

By changing its "corn heads" for a cutting platform, this machine can be used to harvest soybeans. It can be used to harvest and thresh wheat, rice, and sorghum as well.

At left the cutting heads of the John Deere 6600 Combine are shown in the raised position while it unloads corn into a truck.

This John Deere 6600 Corn and Soybean Combine is at work in a cornfield. This model is powered by a 6-cylinder, 110-hp gasoline or diesel engine. It is 19 ft. 10 in. long, 12 ft. 2 in. wide, and 11 ft. 9 in. high. From the rear window of the cab the operator can see the threshed corn accumulating.

Windrower

Making hay while the sun shines is more than an old expression if you're a farmer. It's exactly what this farmer is doing. The windrower she is driving cuts the hay and leaves it behind in rows. The hay will be left out to dry in the sun before it is baled and stored. Otherwise the hay would rot in the barns.

A cutting platform mounted on the front of the windrower cuts 10- to 16-ft. widths, depending on its size and design. The platform floats up and down to follow the contour of the ground. As the windrower moves through the field, a rotating reel pulls the standing hay against the knife blade and then feeds the cut hay into two augers that gather it toward the center of the platform. From there it is forced through two rollers that squeeze out moisture and drop the hay on the ground in rows.

The sounds of the wind and crickets in a hayfield are interrupted by the chugging of an engine. Soon over the horizon a strange-looking machine appears—the International Harvester 275 Windrower with spinning bats flashing in the sun. At the end of the field the operator raises the platform, turns around and lowers it again to cut another swath through the field, leaving row after row of neatly gathered hay behind it. It travels at a little over 9 mph but its knife can cut at the rate of 1,500 strokes per minute. Besides hay, the windrower can harvest alfalfa, grass seed, lentils, green peas, and sorghum.

Backhoe

Watching a backhoe at work is like watching a strange one-armed insect scratching up the earth. Used to dig trenches for laying underground pipes, the backhoe also has a loader attachment in the front. The machine is driven forward to the digging site. There the operator turns his seat around to face the controls and hydraulically drops two stabilizing outriggers, one on each side, to hold the machine in position. The backhoe arm on this Dynahoe 160 can be extended to 18 ft. 6 in. The bucket can dig down as deep as 16 ft. and can even dig back 3 ft. under itself.

Backhoes come in many sizes. Most are mounted on wheels, but some of the larger ones are mounted on tractor-crawler treads. These machines have made it possible to lay networks of underground telephone lines, sewer pipes, water lines, electrical conduits, gas lines, and steam pipes. The success of this machine depends on the intricate but tough hydraulic system it uses to perform the many movements required.

Hydraulic cylinders control every movement of the backhoe. One raises and lowers the boom, one extends and retracts the dipper, one moves the bucket. Two cylinders swing the arm from left to right and two others raise and lower the stabilizers. All this gives the bucket the flexibility to dig, raise, swing, and dump. Different-width buckets are interchangeable. The loader in front uses two cylinders to raise and lower the front bucket and another two to tip it. The engine in this Dynahoe 160 is a 3-cylinder, 90-hp diesel. The machine's total weight is 15,800 lbs.

36

Crane

The two cranes shown here are quite different in design, yet they do the same kind of work at construction sites: pick things up. The 70-ton Bucyrus-Erie Hydrocrane 65-C should be considered as three separate elements. The bottom is the carrier that provides transportation; it has outriggers on both sides to provide a broader base and greater stability for the upper parts. The second element contains its own diesel engine and sits on a revolving frame on the carrier; it contains the pumps, valves, and motors that operate the hoist drums and raise, swing, and lower the boom. The third element is the boom itself, which can be extended from the basic 30 ft. to 200 ft. by the use of insert sections. Smaller additional extensions, or "jibs," can increase the height to 240 ft. The art to operating such a crane is in knowing at what angle to use the boom, how far to swing it, and how much to pick up without tipping the whole thing over.

The smaller 300-C Hydraulic Crane has the advantage of maneuverability in tight construction sites. Three kinds of steering are possible: front wheels only, all four wheels turning together for tight turns, and four wheels "crabbing" or moving at the same angle and in the same direction. The boom, which telescopes from 21 to 51 ft., is mounted with its counterweight on a turntable centered on the chassis. Front and rear outriggers drop down to provide stability.

The Lunar Roving Vehicle is steered by a T-shaped hand-grip control with various forward and reverse speeds. It measures 10 ft. 2 in. long, slightly over 6 ft. wide, and 45 in. high. It weighs 480 lbs. and can carry 1,000 lbs. The wheels are woven zinc-coated piano wire with chevron-shaped titanium treads riveted around the circumference. Each wheel is individually driven by an electric motor powered by two batteries. The two moon photographs were supplied by NASA.

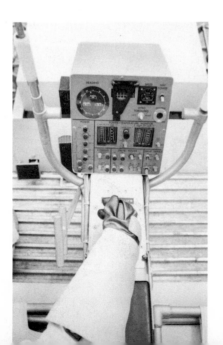

Lunar Rover

The wheel has served man and his machines well in molding and changing the surface of the earth. And now man has stepped on the moon and opened up the universe to space exploration, bringing with him his ancient friend—the wheel.

The Lunar Roving Vehicle was designed to function under the lighter gravitational pull of the moon's surface. It can carry two astronauts with their life-support packs on expeditions to collect lunar samples. They can communicate with each other only through the Lunar Module or earth space-control center. The Rover can travel at 8 mph, cross 28-in. crevasses, climb 25° slopes, and turn in a 20-ft. radius. Because of the limitations of the life-support systems, the Rover's range is limited to 3 miles from the Lunar Module. But new concepts for the Rover's future are being developed. One idea is an unmanned vehicle with a range of over 500 miles that can operate for one year remotely controlled from earth.

Acknowledgments

Thanks go to the many people who helped in the making of this book. Particularly to BARBARA GOODMAN, who wrote, telephoned, and did the leg work for the research, who trudged through the mud and dust of construction sites with me, and who also helped develop and print the photographs.

And to the many others who answered my questions and permitted me to intrude on their time—the machine operators, the foremen, the supervisors, the farmers, and the many company representatives I contacted for information and help. Among them were:

Alice Amideneau
Ed Atkinson, L. B. Smith Metropolitan, Inc.
Jerry Bennet, American Container Line
Lavaugn Boatright, Live Oak Tractor Co.
Carter Busse, Caterpillar Tractor Co.
Roy Chappell, Dixie Farm Equipment Co.
Frank Crosby, Ward Pavements, Inc.

J. P. Daneluk, International Harvester Co.
Louis C. Frank, Terex, division of General Motors
P. J. Gourguechon, Caterpillar of Delaware, Inc.
Paul Greten, Bahls Motor & Implement Co.
Rudy Hilberri, Clark Equipment Co.
William A. Hoffman, Jr., The Hoffman Co.
Joseph D. Jones, L. B. Smith Metropolitan, Inc.
Lee Lanzarotta, International Harvester Co.
A. H. Lavender, National Aeronautics and
   Space Administration
Ray Miller, L. B. Smith Metropolitan, Inc.
Alvin R. Porte
Burton Prince, NASA Tours, TWA
Roland Smith, Phoenix Industries
Phil Stephany, Deere & Co.

And to my family, who would patiently wait in the car while I ran out to shoot a machine working by the road.

About the Author

GEORGE ANCONA is a photographer and filmmaker. Creating this book satisfied a sense of curiosity he has always felt while watching an excavation or construction going on. It also provided an opportunity to spend many hours talking to the men who operate these huge machines. He especially enjoyed the excitement of being in the middle of a construction site watching rumbling monsters roar by throwing up clouds of dust, or watching ships unloading to the squeals of winches and cranes and a chorus of tooting whistles, or standing in the middle of summer cornfields watching combines chew up the crops.

After studying painting in Mexico, Mr. Ancona returned to New York to work for magazines and advertising agencies as an art director. Eventually he turned to photography and began to shoot magazine stories, advertising illustrations, books, and films.

His work has taken him on extensive travels in the United States and abroad, particularly in Latin America.

Today he lives and works in Stony Point, New York. His photographic books include *Faces* and *Bodies,* written by Barbara Brenner, and *Handtalk,* an ABC for the deaf, by Remy Charlip and Mary Beth. He has produced documentaries, industrial, educational, and advertising films, and film sequences for "Sesame Street."